Dear Parents and Educators,

Welcome to Penguin Young Readers! As ⎯⎯⎯⎯⎯⎯
that each child develops at his or her ow⎯⎯⎯⎯⎯⎯
critical thinking, and, of course, reading. ⎯⎯⎯⎯⎯⎯ ⎯⎯⎯⎯⎯ Readers
recognizes this fact. As a result, each Penguin Young Readers book
is assigned a traditional easy-to-read level (1–4) as well as a Guided
Reading Level (A–P). Both of these systems will help you choose the right
book for your child. Please refer to the back of each book for specific
leveling information. Penguin Young Readers features esteemed authors
and illustrators, stories about favorite characters, fascinating nonfiction,
and more!

Max & Ruby: Max's Checkup

LEVEL **2**

GUIDED
READING **G**
LEVEL

This book is perfect for a **Progressing Reader** who:
- can figure out unknown words by using picture and context clues;
- can recognize beginning, middle, and ending sounds;
- can make and confirm predictions about what will happen in the text; and
- can distinguish between fiction and nonfiction.

Here are some **activities** you can do during and after reading this book:
- Make Connections: Doctors give checkups. Which parts of Max's body
  do Doctor Louise and Nurse Ruby want to check? Does your doctor check
  the same body parts?
- Max loves coloring with his markers! Find all the color words in the story.
  Use markers to write each color word in the correct color. For example,
  write the word red using a red marker.

Remember, sharing the love of reading with a child is the best gift
you can give!

—Bonnie Bader, EdM, and Katie Carella, EdM
    Penguin Young Readers program

*Penguin Young Readers are leveled by independent reviewers applying the standards developed by Irene Fountas and Gay Su Pinnell in *Matching Books to Readers: Using Leveled Books in Guided Reading*, Heinemann, 1999.

Penguin Young Readers
Published by the Penguin Group
Penguin Group (USA) Inc., 375 Hudson Street, New York, New York 10014, USA
Penguin Group (Canada), 90 Eglinton Avenue East, Suite 700, Toronto, Ontario M4P 2Y3, Canada
(a division of Pearson Penguin Canada Inc.)
Penguin Books Ltd., 80 Strand, London WC2R 0RL, England
Penguin Group Ireland, 25 St. Stephen's Green, Dublin 2, Ireland (a division of Penguin Books Ltd.)
Penguin Group (Australia), 250 Camberwell Road, Camberwell, Victoria 3124, Australia
(a division of Pearson Australia Group Pty. Ltd.)
Penguin Books India Pvt. Ltd., 11 Community Centre, Panchsheel Park, New Delhi—110 017, India
Penguin Group (NZ), 67 Apollo Drive, Rosedale, Auckland 0632, New Zealand
(a division of Pearson New Zealand Ltd.)
Penguin Books (South Africa) (Pty.) Ltd., 24 Sturdee Avenue,
Rosebank, Johannesburg 2196, South Africa

Penguin Books Ltd., Registered Offices: 80 Strand, London WC2R 0RL, England

Based upon the animated series Max & Ruby
A Nelvana Limited production © 2002–2003

Max & Ruby™ and © Rosemary Wells. Licensed by Nelvana Limited NELVANA™ Nelvana Limited.
CORUS™ Corus Entertainment Inc. All rights reserved. First published in 2010 by Grosset & Dunlap,
an imprint of Penguin Group (USA) Inc. Published in 2011 by Penguin Young Readers, an imprint of
Penguin Group (USA) Inc., 345 Hudson Street, New York, New York 10014. Manufactured in China.

Library of Congress Control Number: 2009031270

ISBN 978-0-448-45376-7   10 9 8 7 6 5 4 3 2 1

PENGUIN YOUNG READERS

LEVEL
PROGRESSING
READER
2

Max & Ruby™

Max's Checkup

Penguin Young Readers
An Imprint of Penguin Group (USA) Inc.

Max was drawing

with his markers.

"Blue!" said Max.

"Louise is coming.

We will play with her

doctor's kit," said Ruby.

Ding-dong!

"Louise is here!"

said Ruby.

"Louise, this can be

our doctor's office,"

said Ruby.

Ruby said,

"I will be the nurse!"

Louise said,

"I will be the doctor!"

The girls looked in the kit.

"This is to hear

a heartbeat!" said Ruby.

"This is to check

inside ears," said Louise.

"We need someone

to be sick," said Ruby.

"Max!" said Louise.

"Max, you need a
checkup," said Ruby.
But Max was not sick.

"Orange!" said Max.

"You can draw later,"

said Ruby.

"Come on, Max!

This will be fun,"

said Ruby.

Louise checked Max's eyes.

"They look okay,"

said Louise.

"Now we need to check

his heart," said Ruby.

"Purple!" said Max.

"You can draw later!"

said Ruby.

She took Max's markers.

Thump-thump,

went Max's heart.

"Sounds good to me,"

said Louise.

"What is next, Doctor?"

asked Ruby.

The girls looked

in their book.

Max tried to leave.

Ruby said, "Come back.

We want to check

your knees."

Louise tapped Max's knee.

Max giggled.

"This is not funny,"

said Ruby.

"Let's check his funny bone,"

said Louise.

She tapped Max's arm.

He didn't laugh.

Ruby said,

"His arm must be broken!"

The girls put Max's arm

in a sling.

"Max, you must

stay in bed!"

said Louise.

Max did not want

to stay in bed.

He wanted to draw.

When the girls were

not looking,

Max got his markers.

Max went to his room.

He took off his sling.

He got out his red marker.

The girls found Max.

"Oh, no!" said Ruby.

"He has chicken pox!"

said Louise.

"Red!" said Max.